Wonderfully Made

UNDER MY BED

no two are the same

one of a kind

Janice Stitziel Bloom

with Marcy Woodcock

unique

special gifts

STORY BOOK 1

DEDICATION

Dedicated to every child who dreams of achieving
—you are a priceless one and only.

May you accomplish more with your gifts
than you ever imagined!

ACKNOWLEDGEMENTS

In loving memory of my Dad, George L. Stitziel,
and in honor of my Mother, Helen L. Stitziel, who taught me the
importance of character—and that in spite of what the world may
say, it's never old-fashioned or out-of-date.
It's important now—today!

To my wonderful husband, who believes in my dreams
and always encourages me to forge ahead,
and to my daughter, who has put the creative
play back into my life—I love you both so very much!

To my talented business partners and Marcy
—without you, these characters would have remained
under my bed and never seen the light of our days,
and I am forever grateful!

Janice Stitziel Bloom
Creator of the Ohmadillapicklearoos

Kristy, Bryan and Jesse were exhausted. They had played soccer earlier that day, and the Dragons had really given their team, the Lightening Bolts, a "run for their money." Coach Joe had assured them that they had done their best, but the trio could not get over losing the game.

"Jesse, you had an awesome shot today; it almost went into the goal," encouraged Kristy.

"Yeah," mumbled Bryan, "I wish I could just get the ball to go towards the goal. I'm just not very good."

"Bryan, don't be so hard on yourself; you'll get there. It takes lots of practice to get the ball into the goal," said Jesse. He didn't want his best buddy to be so discouraged.

"I know," answered Bryan. "But it's just so easy for you; everything is easy for you."

Kristy felt bad for her little brother, but she knew the truth about Bryan. He really wasn't the greatest soccer player; in fact, he might have been the worst player on the team. "Hey guys, let's get some sleep. Mom always says things will look brighter in the morning," she shared as she turned off the light switch.

No sooner had the lights gone out when there was a loud THUMP in the room. All three kids sat up quickly and said, "WHAT WAS THAT?" No one seemed to know. They flicked the light on again and looked around the room. Nothing seemed to be out of place. What could it have been?
Just then Kristy thought to peek under her bed. It was a little dark, but she felt sure she saw something move. She grabbed the lamp on the night stand and shone it under the bed. Then she heard a voice say, "Hey, that light is awfully bright; would you mind not shining it in my face?"

All three children screamed. Bryan and Jesse jumped out of their bed and ran to the door, as Kristy fell over backwards and banged her head on the night stand. "OUCH!" she hollered.

"Oh, I'm so sorry," came the voice from under the bed. "I didn't mean to scare you."

There the voice was again. Bryan and Jesse were on their way out the door, when they remembered Kristy was still on the floor.

"If you would just move that lamp back a little bit so it's not so bright, I would be happy to come out and introduce myself," whispered the voice.

Kristy regained her composure. She pulled the lamp back away from the bed and lifted up the bed skirt, keeping a safe distance. At that moment a small bunny, dressed in a purple plaid jacket and turquoise blue pants, with a tool belt tied around his waist, came hopping out from under the bed. The boys had crawled up on top of the bed; and when they saw the tiny creature, their mouths dropped open, and their eyes became as big as the wheels on Bryan's skateboard.

"Hello," said the cheery little creature. "Please don't be afraid. My name is Mr. George Ohmadillapicklearoo, or you can call me Mr. Oh. I was doing some repairs on my roof. A piece of wood accidentally slid off and went crashing to the ground. I know the loud noise must have really scared you, especially when you were about to fall asleep. I am so sorry; it's no wonder you human beings think that monsters live under your beds, especially when we Dust Bunnies are so careless some times. Please accept my apologies."

The children all looked at each other, not knowing what to think.
Kristy regained her courage. "I'm Kristy, and this is my little brother, Bryan, and our friend Jesse," she said.

"Pleased to meet you, children," said Mr. Oh.

Jesse, feeling brave, spoke up, "Where did you come from, and what are you doing under Kristy's bed?"

"Well," said Mr. Oh, "I came from the Village of Clohverville where I live with my wife and son."

"Clohverville?" questioned Bryan. "Never heard of that; is that around here somewhere?"

"Not exactly," said Mr. Oh. "You've probably never heard of it because. . . (lowering his voice) it's where we *Dust Bunnies* live."

"Dust Bunnies?" said Kristy. "I've heard of dust bunnies before." Kristy thought about it for a minute. "My Gram is always talking about cleaning out the dust bunnies from under her furniture."

"Yes, that's it!" exclaimed Mr. Oh. "We Dust Bunnies live underneath your beds, I in particular, in the Village of Clohverville."

At this point in time, the three children were becoming apprehensive of their new friend; but curiosity got the best of Kristy, and she piped up, "Mr. Oh, if what you are telling us is true, then why don't you take us to visit your village of. . . what did you call it, Cloh. . . ver. . . ?"

"Clohverville," answered Mr. Oh. "I'd be happy to take you for a visit. Clohverville is a wonderful place, and I'm sure my family would love to meet you."

"Okay then," answered Kristy, with a little bit of mischief in her voice. "Let's go." Bryan and Jesse, being boys and always up for an adventure, chimed in, "Yeah, let's do it!"

An excited Mr. Oh said, "This is going to be so much fun. I can't wait for you to see my home and meet my family." With that he instructed the children on what to do.

They laid down on their bellies, side by side, with their arms across each others' backs. Mr. Oh climbed up on Kristy's shoulder. On the count of three, Kristy, Bryan and Jesse closed their eyes and blew three times under the bed. When they opened their eyes, they were in the land of Dust Bunnies, in particular, the Village of Clohverville.

The children thought they
had fallen asleep, and what lay before them was part of a dream; but then their
new friend spoke up, "Welcome to Clohverville, children. You have arrived at a
very special time. Today is Special Gifts Day."

"Special Gifts Day?" questioned Kristy.

"Come on, let's venture into the park and see what's happening," said Mr. Oh.

Everyone has Something to Share

SPE
SH

Kristy, Bryan and Jesse followed Mr. Oh down the path into the area that Mr. Oh referred to as the park. It was a spectacular sight. There were bouquets of balloons with colors from every spectrum of the rainbow. Flags and banners hung from the trees with phrases like: *You're One of a Kind, Do the Best that You Can* and *Everyone Has Something to Share* written on them.

Do the Best that You can

You're One of a Kind

An open field provided a wonderful area for all kinds of sporting activities. The children were so amazed with all the festivities that for a moment they had almost forgotten where they were.

Kristy, being the boldest of the troupe, again asked Mr. Oh, "What is Special Gifts Day?"

Mr. Oh replied, "Kristy, Special Gifts Day is a time when all the bunnies in Clohverville can come together and share something of themselves with the rest of the village. It's something that we look forward to all year."

delicious

"Mr. Oh," asked Jesse, "what do you mean *share something of themselves?*"

"Come, let's take a walk, and I think you will begin to see what I mean," replied Mr. Oh.

The children and Mr. Oh spent the next hour or so wandering through the park. They stopped and visited with bunnies along the way. Each stop they made was a learning experience. Each area was very special, because those bunnies attending that area were sharing something of themselves. No two areas were alike, because no two gifts were alike.

Bryan, amazed by everything, thought. . . *Boy, everyone seems so happy. Is this what it's like to share something of yourself?*

They strolled over to a booth that had little confections all in the shapes of vegetables. There were carrots, of course, green beans, beets, peas and even a few onions. Behind the table stood a lovely lady with a brightly colored dress and a matching flower tucked behind one ear.

Mr. Oh said, "Children, let me introduce you to my lovely wife, Mrs. Oh. Aren't her sweet treats something to behold?"

Mrs. Oh blushed with slight embarrassment and said, "Would you all like to taste one of my sweets?"

"Oh yes!" exclaimed the children.

made with Love

Yum Yum

15

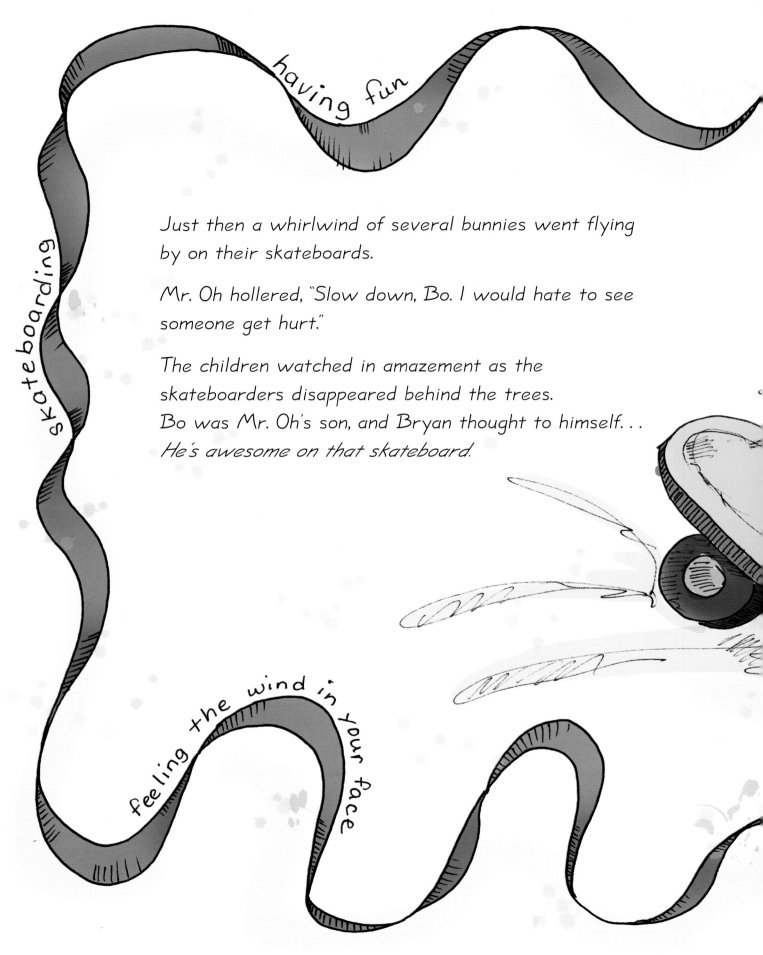

having fun

skateboarding

Just then a whirlwind of several bunnies went flying by on their skateboards.

Mr. Oh hollered, "Slow down, Bo. I would hate to see someone get hurt."

The children watched in amazement as the skateboarders disappeared behind the trees.
Bo was Mr. Oh's son, and Bryan thought to himself. . .
He's awesome on that skateboard.

feeling the wind in your face

17

exciting adventure

doing something you love

giving your best

18

They strolled on to a field where there were bunnies of all ages taking part in several activities. There were soccer and baseball games. Some of the younger bunnies were doing cartwheels and somersaults. One bunny was towering high above the rest as he walked on stilts. It was all a glorious sight to behold. Without thinking, Jesse took off running to join in the soccer game. His friends and Mr. Oh stood and watched him for a while.

"Wow, Jesse is a wonderful soccer player," said Mr. Oh. "Look how he's showing some of the younger bunnies how to pass the ball; he's really sharing something of himself."

Bryan stood there watching and thinking to himself. . . *That is Jesse's special gift. What is it that I can share with others?*

Kristy broke the silence. "Mr. Oh, would you mind if I went back to the area where your wife is making those delicious treats? I love to create, and I bet your wife could teach me some things. "

"That's just fine, Kristy. You go ahead," said Mr. Oh. "Bryan and I will watch Jesse. We'll come and find you when the game is over."

The two sat quietly for a short while until Mr. Oh spoke,
"Bryan, it seems to me that there is something bothering you.
Would you like to talk about it? I'm a really good listener."

Bryan hesitated for a moment and then gave in. "Mr. Oh, I'm just not sure what my special gift is. You see how obvious it is that Jesse is a wonderful soccer player. I play soccer, too, but I'm just not very good. Kristy is always looking for ways to be creative, and she does that very well. . . sometimes a little too well. You should see her bedroom." Mr. Oh laughed. "Mr. Oh," continued Bryan, "how does someone know what their special gift is?"

"I can see you've got a lot on your mind. Let's sit and visit for a while; perhaps talking things through will help," answered Mr. Oh.

Bryan and Mr. Oh sat on the hillside overlooking the fields for quite some time. Mr. Oh began, "Bryan, sometimes we look at other people, and we want to do all the things that they can do; but that's not how we were created. Think about it. If everyone was flowing with creativity or made to be a great soccer player or an awesome skateboard rider, then things would be pretty boring."

Mr. Oh continued to explain to Bryan in some detail that each of us has been given something that we are meant to share with others. And that special gift doesn't have to be something that we do with our hands or feet. Sometimes, it can be the simple way in which we use our words or smile at someone or just listen to what someone else has to say.

one of a kind

No two are the same

Bryan sat quietly for a while and pondered all that Mr. Oh had to say. Just then he heard a loud voice.

"Mr. Oh, hello there, over here, it's me, Looloo." Bryan turned to see a young bunny hobbling along with a crutch to her one side.

"Looloo," responded Mr. Oh, "there you are; I was hoping we might run into you today. Where have you been?"

"I was over in the cabbage patch helping Widow Buttons gather up her cabbage. We needed to take a break from all that picking, so I thought I'd take a walk through town to see what else was happening on Special Gifts Day," she explained. "Who's your friend?" she asked.

Mr. Oh introduced Bryan, and soon Looloo and Bryan were talking to each other like they had been friends for a lifetime. Bryan got lost in the conversation with Looloo and never once glanced again at the soccer game. Before he knew it the game was over, and Jesse had joined them.

It was getting pretty late, and Mr. Oh thought it was probably time for them to find Kristy and get the children back home. Bryan was feeling so comfortable talking with Looloo that he hated to leave. Looloo said that she needed to get back to Widow Buttons anyway, and that she'd better get going. She started towards Widow's house, stopped and turned around.

"Bryan," she said. "it was so much fun to visit with you. Thanks for sharing your special gift of friendship. Please come and visit us again."

Bryan blushed a bit and then waved to his new friend. He sat for a minute thinking about what Looloo had said. "Mr. Oh, is being friendly really a gift?" he asked.

"Yes, it is. And it's one of the best gifts of all. Bryan, you are wonderfully made, and you definitely have something very special about yourself to share." Mr. Oh smiled and could see a smile come over Bryan's face. "Come on; let's go find your sister."

For the first time since they started on this adventure, Bryan felt something different take place in his heart. All the feelings of wanting to be like Jesse or someone else faded away, and he knew that he would never be the same. Bryan did have something to offer, his "Special Gift of Friendship," and he couldn't wait to get back home.

"Friendship is the only cement that will ever hold the world together."

Woodrow Wilson

Ohmadillapicklearoos

Those Villager Dust Bunnies Under My Bed™

Mrs. Oh   Loo Loo   Bo Oh

"Story books with a purpose!"

"Endearing Cast of Characters"

"A Must Read for all Children"

"Every story includes character traits that can be taught year-round."

"The series…"

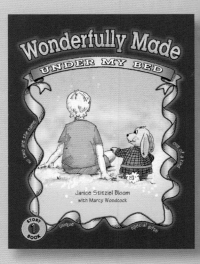

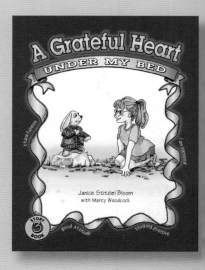

Ohmadillapicklearoos Action Guides

Book Summary

Bryan is frustrated. He is the worst player on his soccer team. Why can't he be as good a soccer player as his friend Jesse? He even wonders if he has any special talent at all to share with others.

With the help from the villager dust bunnies who just happen to live under the bed, Bryan learns that everyone has a special talent. . . a gift that is meant to be shared with others.

"Perfect for use in the classroom!"

"Activities, projects and adventures designed by a professional educator."

"Engaging materials kids will love."

"Fun and interesting activities allow children to connect the stories to real life!"

"***Easy*** to use for teachers and parents."

To order Ohmadillapicklearoos storybooks or accompanying action guides, visit our Web site at *www.VillagerDustBunnies.com,* call us at *1-877-641-8679* or email us at info@villagerdustbunnies.com

Additional storybooks in the series will be available soon.

Group sales, package deals, and on-line resources are all available! Order the entire Ohmadillapicklearoo storybook series today… a team member will be glad to help you!

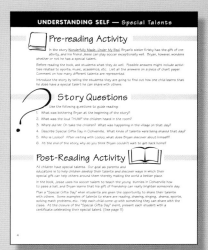

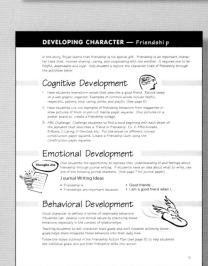

Villager book publishing™

Villager Book Publishing
An imprint of Synergistic Strategies, Inc.
P. O. Box 4629
Cedar Hill, Texas 75106-4629

For more information about Villager Book Publishing's products, group orders, additional activities to use with children or the Ohmadillapicklearoos Series, visit www.VillagerDustBunnies.com, call us at 1-877-641-8679 or email us at info@villagerdustbunnies.com.

Library of Congress Control Number 2007931436

ISBN 13   978-1-934643-00-6
ISBN 10   1-934643-00-9

First hardcover printing, August 2007

All illustrations hand drawn by Marcy Woodcock
Graphic art provided by Don A. Fischer, Fischer Creative